High-Frequency READERS™

I Like

Written by Gay Su Pinnell

Illustrated by Lauren Scheuer

Scholastic Inc.

New York Toronto London Auckland Sydney
Mexico City New Delhi Hong Kong

ISBN 0-439-13187-1

12 11 10

Printed in China

5/0
62

I like to wake up.

I like to eat.

I like to read.

I like to write.

I like to ride.

I like to hug.

I like to sleep.